Top 15 EPIC Minecraft Building Ideas to Impress Your Friends!

(Minecraft House Ideas Guide)

Minecraft does not need any introduction. The incredible popularity and infinite fans of this sandbox indie game says it all. Minecraft is a not any ordinary building game. What makes is so infamous and highly addictive is that it allows you to build almost anything you want. Minecraft gives you a chance to turn your imaginations into creations, which includes making houses as well.

Building houses and shelters is the main and most interesting part of Minecraft. You can make any types of houses you want. It could be a tree house, a lava house, an emergency shelter, house under water, house in the sky, mushroom house, temples, forts, your dream castle and much more.

While the list of what types of buildings and houses you can make in Minecraft is endless, following are step by step procedures of some of the most popular type of Minecraft houses.

Let's Start With a Simple House…

The first and the easiest to make is a small simple house. It offers you shelter and safety against the deadly mobs.

Step 1: To build a house in Minecraft, you need a couple of tools and materials. You can make all the required things yourself.

First make a crafting bench with four wooden planks

Place three wooden planks in the top row and two stick in the remaining centre grids of the crafting table to make a wooden pickaxe. You will need this tool to gather stones.

Now use your wooden pickaxe to mine stone blocks and obtain stones. You will need at least 12 stones to craft the remaining required tools.

Put two sticks and three stones in the crafting table to make the stone pickaxe. The placement would be the same as you did while crafting wooden pickaxe. Here the stone blocks would assume the place the wooden planks.

Next, make a stone axe by placing two sticks and three stone blocks in the crafting table, as illustrated in the image below. The ingredients are same, only the placement is different.

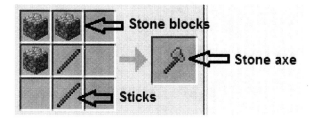

Next, make a stone shovel. To do so, craft one stone block and two sticks vertically in the middle column. The stone block should be placed on the top slot.

Step 2: Now that you have crafted the required tools, next step is to decide what type of material you want your house to be made of. Though your house is your shelter, it is still vulnerable to enemy attacks and deadly explosions. Your selection will determine how safe you and your house are from all such disasters.

You can select from the following building material.

Wood

Wood is the most common and easiest-to-obtain source of building material. However, it is flammable and can be accessed by the mob of creepers. You can get wood blocks by cutting down trees. Use your stone axe to cut trees. You need about 70 – 100 wooden blocks to build a simple small house.

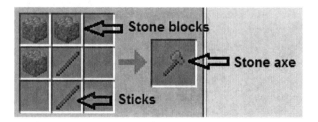

Dirt

You can also dirt to make your house. It is inflammable but just like wood, it is vulnerable to creeper attacks.

Brick Blocks

Brick blocks have the power to resist creeper attacks. However, it is very hard to obtain. To make brick block, first you need to gather bricks. Bricks can be obtained by smelting clay and coal in a furnace, as shown in the image below.

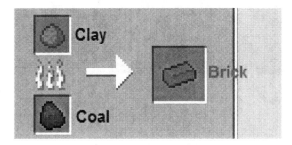

Furnace is mostly found in NPC villages or you can also craft it with eight cobblestones. Once you get the bricks, put them in the crafting table to get brick blocks. Four bricks when placed in the following illustrated manner makes one brick block.

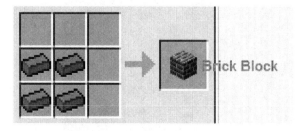

To build a house of bricks, you need approximately one hundred brick blocks. It implies you would have to obtain at least 400 bricks.

Sandstone

If you are making a house in desert, you can also use sandstone. Four pieces of sand compressed out into one block of sandstone.

Cobblestone

Cobblestone is the perfect building material. It has the highest level of resistance. There are three ways to obtain cobblestones.

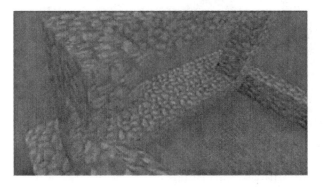

Cobblestones naturally appear in dungeons and NPC villages. You need to find and mine them.

You can build an infinite cobblestone generator.

You can obtain cobblestones by combining water and lava.

Sand or Gravel

You should never use sand or gravel in the construction of your house. These two materials are highly affected by gravity. You won't be able to make a roof out of either of them plus the four wall shelter made out of them can be destroyed easily by just one creeper explosion.

Step 3: Now that you all the required tools and building materials, let's get on to making your house. First you need to build the walls of your house. Make at least 4 blocks high walls, with house size 7 x 7 and a door in the middle.

Step 4: Build the roof of your house. Smelt some sand in a furnace to make lights and windows. Add at least four windows 2 x 2 each.

Step 5: Light your house with torches. You can make your own torch by crafting a coal or red stone above a stick. Lights and torches scare away the mobs. The more lit your house it, the more you are safe in it.

Step 6: Put wooden planks in a 3 x 2 position to make the front door.

Voila! You just created your first house in Minecraft. Decorate it with colors, mushrooms, TV, automatic piston doors etcetera.

The first two steps, crafting tools and building materials, remains the same in all types of houses.

How to Make a Big House in Minecraft

The procedure to build a huge house in Minecraft is more or less the same, as the simple house building process. The difference is mainly in the dimensions of the house plus the huge one contains a few modern placements.

Step 1: Build a huge base for your huge house. It should be made up of at least 30 blocks. You can use any material of your choice.

Step 2: Erect 10 blocks high walls around the base frame. Likewise, build the inside walls.

Step 3: Make the roof of your house. You can either make a simple straight roof that just connects the walls. Or you can make a pointed roof by putting steps on both sides. Put the next

step higher than the previous one until both sides meet at the top. Cover the remaining gaps.

Step 4: Put doors in your house. If you have extra building material, then make double doors. They look more aesthetic. If you are playing the hard difficulty level, then use iron to make doors as wooden doors can be easily broken by zombies.

Step 5: Use glowstone and redstones to make torches. Make sure your entire house, especially the exterior is well lit to save your house from mob spawning and explosions.

Step 6: To add windows, dig 2 x 2 holes in the front of your house. Fit the glass windows in these holes. You can make glass by smelting sand in the furnace.

Step 7: Dig the floor space and place blocks in it. Finally, add a crafting table, chairs, furnace, bed, chest and TV in your house.

How to Build a Medieval Style House in Minecraft

To make a huge medieval style house in Minecraft, you need to have the following items in your inventory.

84 wooden planks

125 wood logs

75 white wool – Kill a sheep or right click a sheep with shears to obtain white wool

46 stone bricks

1 Netherrack (also known as Netherstone)

1 door (2 wooden planks to make a door)

5 torches

116 wooden stairs – Wooden stairs can be created by placing 6 wooden planks on the crafting table, in the following manner. Six planks make four stairs.

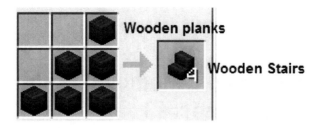

Wooden planks

Wooden Stairs

8 stone brick stairs – Stone brick stairs are crafted the same way as the wooden stairs. You just need to replace the wooden planks with stone bricks.

Stone bricks

Stone brick stairs

4 stone brick slabs – Stone brick can be crafted with 3 stone bricks, placed in the following illustrated manner. 3 pieces of stone bricks yields 6 stone brick slabs.

6 stone brick slabs

stone bricks

22 glass panes – Glass panes can be crafted with 6 glass blocks, placed in the following

illustrated manner. 6 pieces of glass yields 16 glass panes.

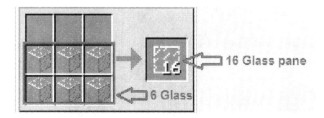

Now that you have gathered the required inventory, follow the below mentioned steps to make your medieval style house.

Step 1: Clear up a 7 x 9 space for the base of the house.

Step 2: Surround the space with wooden logs and white wool, as illustrated in the following image. Make 3 block high walls with these items. Make sure to leave a space in the white wool walls for the windows.

Step 3: Fit the glass panes in the window spaces.

Step 4: Make the wooden floor as shown in the image below.

Step 5: Make a 3 x 3 fireplace using stone bricks. Place a stone brick slab in the bottom-middle of the fireplace. At the back row, place one more stone brick and a stone brick stair on either side of it.

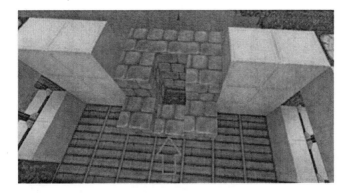

Step 6: Place two more stone bricks, one on each side of the middle row.

Step 7: Place one more stone brick at the front row of the fireplace. Add a stone brick stair on either side of it.

Step 8: Place some more wooden logs to make the second floor of your house. Make sure the second layer of logs quay out he first one, as shown below.

Step 9: Make wooden floor of the second floor. Make sure to leave a four block space for the stairs.

Step 10: Make the walls of the second floor just like you made the first floor wall. Leave space for windows. Insert glass panes in the window space.

Step 11: Repeat step 5 – 7 to make fireplace on the second floor.

Step 12: Make arches with wool and wooden logs, on either side of the house.

Step 13: Using stone bricks, erect a two floor high cross on top of the fireplace to make the chimney.

Step 14: Use the wooden chairs to make the roof of your house.

Step 15: Surround the chimney with stone brick stairs.

Step 16: Cover the stone brick stairs with stone brick slabs.

Step 17: Put a block of stone brick inside the chimney. Light a torch on top of the block.

Step 18: To light up the fireplace, put a Netherrack in the hole of the first floor fireplace. Use flint and steel to burn it.

Step 19: Add stairs descending from the second floor to the first floor.

Step 20: Line up the remaining torches in the inside of the roof of second floor.

Step 21: Finally, place the wooden door at the entrance.

How to Build a Treehouse in Minecraft

Step 1: Cut out a wide and high hollow tube from the tree, that has not yet been converted into wooden planks.

Step 2: Place ladder to climb up and down the tube. Wrap a wooden plank shack round the tube. Make sure to dig holes for door in the shack.

Step 3: Build bridges that connects it to the other shacks.

Step 4: Add support beams in the end.

Step 5: If you want to make a high tree house, add extra floors by extending the size of the tube. Repeat step 2 to 4 for building the other floors. Finally, place a bed, book shelf, paintings and other furniture in your tree house.

How to Build a Slaughter House in Minecraft

Step 1: Clear up a 15 x 15 space for the slaughter house. Surround it by cobblestones.

Step 2: Erect a 4 blocks high walls around it.

Step 3: At the back side of the base, expand a five blocks base and connect them as illustrated in the image below.

Step 4: Erect an eight blocks high wall surrounding the total base.

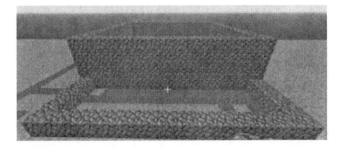

Step 5: Make the roof of the house by adding five-block layers, each overlapping the other.

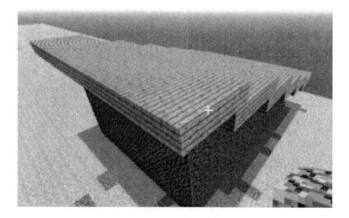

Step 6: Make the front entrance, enter through it, walk straight to the other side and make the back entrance.

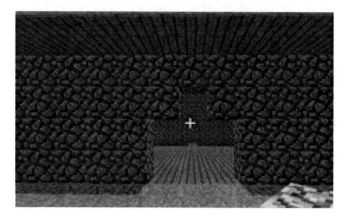

Step 7: Add wooden stairs in the corner of the room. Finally, add a window in the top floor.

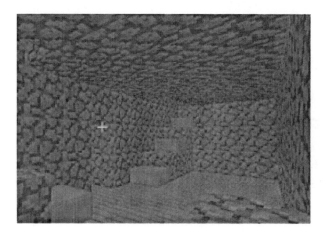

How to Build a Safe Shelter in Minecraft

Minecraft is addictive. However, this addiction of yours can end soon if you do not take appropriate measures to protect yourself from the deadly mobs. It is very important to build a safety shelter as to enjoy prolonged bouts of the amazing Minecraft.

Well, you don't really have to make an entirely different safe shelter. Just a couple of modifications to your house and it will become a safe shelter.

Follow the steps explained below to convert your house into a safety shelter.

Step 1: First and most important, replace the wooden doors of your house with iron doors. Wooden doors are no protection against zombies; they can easily invade your house through the wooden doors.

Step 2: Place as many as torches as possible, both inside and outside the house. Lights prevent the mobs from spawning.

Step 3: Erect three block high walls around your house. Add another over-hanging block layer to prevent spider invasion.

Step 4: Create a trench of water around your house. Flowing water drowns the mobs.

Step 5: Dig a deep hole under the outer corner of the trench to flush out the trapped and drowned mobs. Also, set up a redstone trapdoor bridge over the trench.

Step 6: Build a watchtower on the roof to keep a check on the mobs.

Step 7: Create a secret bunker under your house as your safety escape. Keep the bunker well equipped with weapons, armor, torches and food. Escape to the bunker as soon as the mobs invade your house.

Step 8: Dig a secret underground tunnel in the bunker that takes you out of the house. This will be your safety exit.

Step 9: If your house is vulnerable to Endermen who transfuse into the base of the house, add a couple of flood gates to flush them out of your shelter.

How to Build a Mushroom House in Minecraft

Mushroom houses are very comfortable to live in and are also very easy to build.

To make your own mushroom house, you need the following items.

Building blocks

Ladder

Red mushroom – Mushrooms are mostly found in dark places

Bone meal - Bone meal can be crafted by putting one bone in the center middle grid of the crafting table. One piece of bone crafts out three bone meals.

Torch

Mushroom house is one of the easiest and quickest houses to build.

Step 1: Use the bone meal to grow the red mushroom on the ground. The grown up mushroom should be about 5 x 5 x 6.

Step 2: Make a three block trunk beneath the mushroom and attach a ladder to it.

Step 3: Build the floor of the mushroom house. You can use any building material of your choice.

Step 4: Place a torch inside to light up your mushroom house.

Step 5: Put a small bed, a chest and a crafting table inside the house.

How to Build Your Dream Castle in Minecraft

Castles are safest place to live. They contain everything you need to survive in the Minecraft city.

Step 1: Select a location for your castle. Flat mountain tops are the ideal place for building castles.

Step 2: If you cannot find a flat location or your chosen location is very hilly, flatten it out a bit.

Step 3: Carve an outline of the walls of your castle. Leave room for expansion, if you intend to so later on.

Step 4: Make a map of your castle. Plan out the placement of rooms, kitchen, courtyard etc.

Step 5: Erect the outer wall of your castle, with cobblestones. Make sure to leave space for windows.

Step 6: Fit glass panes in the window space.

Step 7: Build the over head roof. Add an overhang to prevent spiders from invading your house.

Step 8: Add iron doors at the entrance.

Step 9: Build a small tower next to the main castle. Connect the two structures with a common wall.

Step 10: Build another tower, larger than the previous one on the other, on the other side of the main castle. Build the floor, ceiling, roof, staircase and fireplace. Make sure both the towers contain iron door.

Step 11: Add as many floors as you want. Make sure to add a safe bunker underground.

Decorate the castle as you like. Here are a few tips to do that.

Make the kitchen countertop with stone bricks. Add a refrigerator and a furnace.

Dig a wide hole and insert a few pistons in it to make a large table. Around the pistons, place a few chairs.

Put a wooden stair block and attach two signs on either side of it, as armrests.

To make a rug, place different colored blocks in the center of the main room, in any pattern.

Put two small beds side by side to make a double bed and place a crafting table on both sides. Place a chest at the foot of the bed.

Build a book shelf next to the fireplace.

To decorate the exterior of the castle, place fence blocks at all corners of the towers.

To make flower vases, place two dirt boxes and surround them with trap doors. Spread some flowers on top of the dirt boxes. Make as many flower vases as you want and put them in different places, inside and outside the castle.

How to Build a High Rise Tower in Minecraft

Step 1: Gather at least 15 stacks of whatever building blocks you intend to use.

Step 2: Erect as high a tower as you want. You can add more stacks to increase the height of the tower.

Step 3: Top it off with a circle and them leap off. Don't worry you won't die forever. Click **Respawn** and go back to your tower.

Step 4: Finish building up your tower.

Step 5: Add a ladder next to the tower, place a door at the entrance and a drawbridge.

Decorate it as you like. Stand on top of your own high rise tower and enjoy the scenic view of the Minecraft city.

How to Make Cave Home in Minecraft

If you could not find any suitable location for your dream house, do not have much inventory and building material, or need to make a house immediately; then a cave is the perfect place to start with. Most of them are already well lit. You do not need to erect walls, floor and roof as all these are already present in the cave. Since the basic structure is already there, building of a cave requires very less material.

You just need to renovate the cave to make it your instant home.

Here is what you need to do to build a home out of a cave.

Step 1: Find a cave, if you don't have one currently. Caves are mostly found on sea shores and sides of mountains.

Step 2: There are normally deadly mobs in almost every cave. You need to kill them first in order to invade the cave. Gather some weapons, torches, sword, food, axe and wood blocks before you enter any newly found cave.

Step 3: Walk about a hundred blocks straight into the cave and put torches there. Light up the entire cave. Kill any mobs that come in your way.

Step 4: Time to explore the cave! Seal every exit, opening and even a small hole that you find after hundred blocks to prevent the deadly mobs and monsters from invading the cave.

Step 5: Seal the front entrance of the cave and place a door there. Add some windows in the walls of the cave.

Step 6: Add paintings, furniture and whatever you want to decorate your cave home.

Once you are done with the hundred block cave, start opening and conquering the sealed exits one by one to expand your cave house.

How to Make a Nether Portal in Minecraft

Nether is the most dangerous area of Minecraft. It is full of deadly monsters, ghosts and zombies. Now the question is why anyone would ever want to visit such a deadly place. Well, while Nether is an extremely dangerous place, it does not contain creepers. Skeletons appear very rare and that even to play with wither skeletons.

Nether is home to some of those items. It contains netherrack which is the best stone to light in a fireplace. Netherrack if flamed correctly burns forever. Then there is soul sand, which is used in making lures and traps. Nether quartz ore can only be found in the Nether.

Nether has so much to offer that the risks and hazards in living there are definitely worth the benefits.

There are two ways of making a Nether Portal; with and without obsidian blocks.

To make a nether portal with obsidian blocks,

Step 1: Gather 14 blocks of obsidian – Obsidian is the strongest block in Minecraft. Obsidian is made when water hits a lava stream. Therefore it is mostly found deep below the sea level near lava beds. You need a diamond pickaxe to mine

Obsidian blocks Mining takes about fifteen seconds. At times, obsidian is also found in village chests.

Step 2: Erect a frame of the portal using the obsidian blocks. Build two pillars, each containing stack of five obsidian blocks. The pillars should be placed two blocks apart each other. Connect the pillars by placing the remaining four blocks in the two block space between the pillars. Put two on top and two on bottom of the space.

If you don't have enough Obsidian blocks, you can replace the corner four blocks with dirt or any other building blocks.

Step 3: Next you need to obtain flint and steel, in order to light the portal. To make flint and steel, you need one iron ingot and one piece of flint.

Flint can be obtained by mining gravel. You can also get it from the villagers in exchange of emeralds.

To make flint and steel, place both the items on the crafting table, in the following illustrated manner.

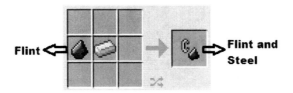

Step 4: Now that you have obtained the flint and steel, light the portal with it. While this is the best method to light up the Nether portal, you can also use lava and two blocks of wood for the same purpose.

If you are using flint and steel, then your portal will become purple after lighting.

Step 5: Stand at the center of the obsidian and wait for a while. Your screen will pop up a welcome notice saying "entering the nether". Go ahead and walk inside your newly made Nether portal.

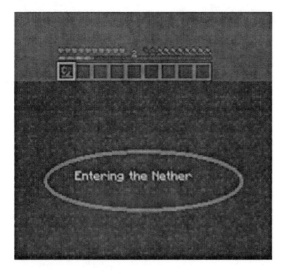

To make a nether portal without obsidian blocks,

Step 1: First you need to gather lava equivalent to 14 blocks, contained in a bucket and another bucket of water.

Step 2: Use dirt to mold a 1 x 4 trench for the base of the portal.

Step 3: Fill the trench with lava blocks and top it up with water. If you followed the process correctly, the trench will turn into obsidian.

Step 4: Increase the height of the frame by making three more dirt molds in the upward direction. Repeat the same process to turn the molds into obsidian. Similarly, make the top trench to connect the pillars.

Step 5: Remove the excess dirt and lighten up your nether portal.

Note: This process for making nether portal is not applicable if you are in Nether already. This is because over there you will have to water to top up the lava filled trenches. This method is appropriate for making portal by the mountain side, rather than on the ground.

How to Build a Temple in Minecraft

Step 1: Find a suitable location and mark a boundary for your temple. Erect a furnace on any of the corners.

Step 2: Use cobblestones to make the base of the temple, snow block forms to make the boundary and smooth stone forms to make the checked – pattern floor space as shown in the image below.

Step 3: Fill in the floor space gaps with dark grey wool and half-height smooth stones. Make sure the smooth stones slightly overlap the snow stones boundary

Step 4: Make eight columns with light and dark grey wools. A total of nine layers of light grey wool are required to complete the columns.

Step 5: Top up the columns with dark grey wool caps.

Step 6: Connect all the columns with smooth stones. Attach the stone connecting bridge from the second wool from the top of all the columns, as shown below.

Step 7: Build cap on top of every column, using snow stones.

Step 8: Add another layer of snow stone cap, this one slightly smaller than the first layer.

Step 9: Add a thick layer of snow block square to connect the small snow stone caps. Leave small holes in the square to show the depth and volume of columns.

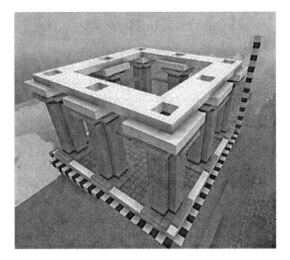

Step 10: Build another layer of snow block squares smaller than and atop the previous one, in the following illustrated manner.

Step 11: Double the large snow stone square with a layer of smooth stones. Form two layers of yellow wool, one next the cobblestone square and another atop the small snow stone square. You can obtain yellow wool by placing white wool and dandelion yellow in the middle grids of crafting table.

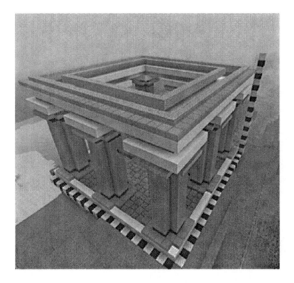

Step 12: Top up the large yellow wool square with green wool. Add another square of green circle slightly smaller than the small yellow wool square. You can obtain green wool by placing white wool and cactus green in the middle grids of crafting table.

Step 13: Use cobblestones to make a small room for ladder.

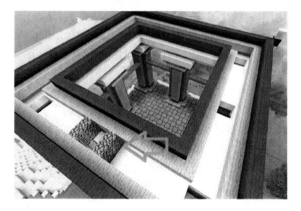

Step 14: Add one more layer of green wool, slightly smaller than the previous larger one. Top it up with dirt. Leave a space where you have placed the ladder.

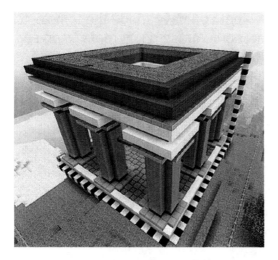

Step 15: Finally, close the roof with wool of any color. Here we have used green color to make the roof. You can also use a mix of colors to make a pattern on the roof. Make sure not to close the ladder opening.

Step 16: Now that you have made the temple, it is time to grow some grass on its roof. To do so, you need to make a stair case with dirt block, ascending from the grass on the ground to the dirt part of the roof.

Step 17: To make the water column, dig a small hole in the centre of the roof. Build a collecting pool right under it.

Step 18: Decorate the inner side of the roof with glass and glow stones.

Step 19: Add a door from where the ladder to the roof starts.

Step 20: Decorate the roof by replacing a few smooth stone blocks with wool of any color. Here we have used green color wool to match with the echo friendly theme of the temple.

How to Build Ruins in Minecraft

Ruins give an ancient aura which makes the game even more adventurous. And the best part is that you don't have to look for a location and build the ruins from scratch. You can do this if you want to, however an easier approach is to turn a part of your house into ruins.

Step 1: Ruins are all about ancient structures and cracked stones. To make ruins out of your house, first you need to create a mix of stone blocks with cracked stones. The best combination for creating ruins is of cobblestones, stone bricks and cracked stone bricks.

Step 2: There is nt hard and fast rule for making ruins. Just replace about half of the existing blocks of the building with both blocks and cracked bricks. Placement of the blocks is completely at your discretion. You can make layers of cracked bricks, or cracked pillars or can go for just random placement.

Step 3: Once you are done with the structure, hang some vines from the roof. Spread a few shrubs, wild grass, dead bushes and cobwebs around the structure.

Step 4: Breaks a few blocks from any wall and place them randomly on the ground next to the broken wall.

Step 5: Place a couple of torches to lighten up your ruins.

Final Words

A House is the most important requirement in Minecraft. And making a variety of houses is the most interesting part in this game. You build a house and you will feel a real sense of accomplishment.

Well, now you are all set to build your own world in the city of Minecraft. Let your creativity flow, make a mind map of your next building venture, grab the ingredients, build your house, decorate it and make your dream come true.

CPSIA information can be obtained at www.ICGtesting.com
Printed in the USA
LVOW07s1454160315

430764LV00020B/1105/P